Pilgrims and Poltergeists
Volume I

Witches Brew

&

Mother Crewe

Legends & True Tales

From Olde Plymouth

By

Diane L. Finn

The Tin Lantern Press

Plymouth, MA

Library of Congress Catalog Card Number

ISBN: 978-0-692-87858-3

Third Edition June 2023

The Tin Lantern Press

P.O. Box 3541

Plymouth, MA 02361

Tel: 774 320 5132

Email: thetinlanternpress@gmail.com

Printing: The Country Press, Inc.

To: *Vicki, Joyce & Barbara*
who made
Aunt Rachel, Witch Hazel
and Mother Crewe
come to life.

Acknowledgements

Special thanks to:

Molly Wilson, Illustrator.
Pat Cotta, Editor.
Mike Manzi, Computer Guru.

Joyce & Barb for the late night reviews of the stories and the project.

Nancy Gratta, Angels by the Sea, for her inspirational courses and programs.

Bill Finn, son, for his coaching and support to turn obstacles into possibilities through the technology of the Landmark Education, Advance Communication Course.

Erin Finn Zell for her constant love and support.

And my husband Dan for his vision and skill in the creation of Colonial Lantern Tours leading to the discovery of these amazing stories.

~Contents~

~ Introduction ~

In the 17th century, in every European country, kings, religious leaders, nobles and peasants all had a belief in witches and witchcraft. Those who settled in New England brought those ideas and superstitions with them.

When for what seemed like no logical reason, friends or neighbors became ill, livestock or crops were destroyed, grain became mildew, or milk, ale, and wine turned sour, the community believed it was caused by evil beings. Therefore, it was most important to protect a person, home, and community from practitioners of this evil.

As early as 1641, in the New England colonies, witchcraft was punishable by death. Many practices evolved to either protect the home or goods from these supposed evil ones or identify the person causing the community such mischief.

When someone was accused or convicted of "compacting with the devil," it was the duty of the magistrates to take action to punish and destroy this evil.

Much attention about witches has been paid to Salem and Boston, but few know of the two witch trials that took place here in the Plymouth Courts.

When it comes to witch legends, the stories of Mother Crewe, Bethia Hazel's Revenge and Aunt Rachel's Curse have entertained participants on the Plymouth Colonial Lantern Tours for many years. The first two were adapted from the books written by Jane Goodwin Austin in the 1890's. Aunt Rachel's Curse was first related to me by a Plimoth Plantation Pilgrim. With some research, I eventually found the story in more than one source.

Historians claim that most of these characters and events are fictional. I have been on a search to connect and confirm some of the pieces of this puzzle, since many of the places, people and graves **did** exist.

It is clear to me that Jane exaggerated the details and often merged specific events or characters to dramatize the story.

However, Ms. Austin claims, "The story of Mother Crewe's curse, with its results, is substantially true, and the scene depicted in Chapter xliv (Mother Crewe's Last Curse) is literally so. The tragedy embodied in Chapter xxiv (A Day of Terror) is also a matter of history..."

I believe her...do you?

Diane Finn October, 2016

Legends of Witches in Plymouth

1740 – 1780

Tales of Mother Crewe

by Karen White and Diane Finn
Adapted from Dr. LeBaron and His Daughter
Written by Jane Goodwin Austin

Cast of Characters:

Characters in Jane Goodwin Austin's book

Elizabeth Crewe - Main character in the legend, considered by many to be a witch.

Bathsheba Crewe - Elizabeth's daughter, a teenager.

Ansel Ring - Fiancé of Bathsheba.

Molly Peach Best friend of Bathsheba.

Ansel Jr. (Jack), Acsah, Yetmercy, Ichabod
Children of Ansel & Molly.

Acsah Ring -Daughter of Ansel & Molly who marries a sailor.

Ichabod English - Husband of Acsah.

Molly, Nettie, Dorcas, newborn
Children of Acsah & Ichabod

Characters in the story whose graves are on Burial Hill

Consider Howland 1699-1759 Father of Thomas S. Howland.

Thomas S. Howland 1734-1779 Cursed by Mother Crewe.

Hannah Howland 1754 – 1780 - Thomas Southworth Howland's sister in love with Ansel (Jack) Ring.

 Dr. Francis LeBaron 1668-1704 - Famous Plymouth doctor originally from France, whose sons and grandsons went to Harvard and became doctors.

Lazarus Le Baron 1698-1773 -The doctor who came to visit Bathsheba Crewe. Son of Dr. Francis LeBaron.

Dr. Isaac Le Baron 1743-1819 Son of Dr. Lazarus LeBaron.

Chapter 1 – The Betrayal

Dr. Lazarus LeBaron rode swiftly toward his destination astride his horse, Pegasus. He barely noticed the beauty of the fall foliage, as his concentration was on his patients. He was surprised to see Ansel just ahead. He expected him to be by his fiancé's side.

"Ansel, Ansel Ring, halt!" he shouted. "How is Bathsheba, your bride-to-be, doing today?"

To the doctor's surprise, Ansel replied," I don't know. I'm on my way to her house now."

"Well, so am I," said Dr. LeBaron. "She is a mighty sick girl, Ansel. You and Mother Crewe must stay watch over her all this night. I have brought some medicine to ease the pain and let her have a restful sleep."

Approaching the Crewe home in Plympton, Dr. LeBaron noticed how shabby the cottage looked, even with the golden glowing hue of the setting sun. Inside, the curtains were dingy and the house unkempt. Certainly tending to the sick was a difficult, draining task, but still this was little more than a hovel.

Standing over the pale, limp body of the sickly girl was her best friend, Molly Peach. As the doctor and Ansel entered the room, Dr. LeBaron could not help but notice the look that passed between the young man and the beautiful blonde girl whose cheeks reflected her name.

Suddenly, the door flew open, and the sickly girl's mother entered. She was bent over, with a shock of wild, wooly, gray hair, her posture and appearance that of a bitter widow aged well beyond her years. Her eyes were sunken in their sockets, with dark circles beneath. Some of her teeth were missing due to neglect, and her clothes were tattered and stained. The sight of her caused Dr. LeBaron to shiver.

"Mother Crewe, you have a very sick child here. It is important that she receives this medicine. You and Ansel take turns keeping watch by her side all through the night. I will stop by again tomorrow evening to see how she is faring."

"Molly, you should go to bed and get some rest," the doctor advised. He had more concern for the new relationship he saw brewing than for Molly's well-being. With that, Dr. Lazarus LeBaron departed for Plymouth.

Molly took the medicine into the next room to prepare. She pulled Ansel aside and whispered, "Look at

Bathsheba. She is so delirious, she will sleep all night. I'll put the potion in Mother Crewe's cider, that will knock her out, and we can spend the evening together. After all the long hours we spent tending to our friend, we deserve a night off. Who will ever know, and what harm can come?"

Ansel was weak in spirit. The thought of an evening with the beautiful, young maiden was more than he could bear, and he reluctantly agreed to her devious plan.

As Molly predicted, the potion soon worked on Elizabeth Crewe, and she slumped over the bed of Bathsheba while the couple stole away hand-in-hand to the next room by the hearth. Ansel's guilt was soon melted away by warm, tender kisses, and the hours passed quickly.

At about 2 a.m. Bathsheba awoke shivering almost uncontrollably. Her body was racked with pain. As she tried to move her feet, she felt a heavy weight upon them, and awoke enough to see the figure of her mother slumped over her bed. In a hoarse whisper she tried to arouse the woman, but to no avail. In the distance, she could hear whispering, and laughter. The voices sounded so familiar. She called out, but no one answered. With all the strength she could muster, Bathsheba dragged herself from her sick bed. Inching her way along the shabby walls, she pulled her body to the adjoining room. There on a bench by the hearth, she spied the couple.

Her fiancé and her best friend in an embrace of passionate kisses stabbed at Bathsheba's heart as sharp as any knife could penetrate. "TRAITORS," she screamed and collapsed on the floor.

Her screech woke Mother Crewe. She ran to the room and knew in her heart what had happened. She and Ansel carried Bathsheba to her bed. Mother Crewe drove the betrayers out into the night, and they left in the shame and horror of their evil deed.

Chapter 2 – The Curse

Bathsheba died three days later from her illness, and her broken heart. Of course, her mother blamed the couple for the tragic death of her only child.

About a week after her death, Ansel and Molly appeared at Rev. Leonard's parsonage on Leyden Street in Plymouth looking to be married. The pastor knew that Ansel had been betrothed to Bathsheba, and was very surprised to see the young couple at his door so soon after Bathsheba's death. He turned them away.

Three weeks later they wound up at Judge Lothrop's (Justice of the Peace) located at the top of North Street. And so the couple was wed. After a brief sermon from the judge advising them to "take heed, lest a bad beginning should bring about a worse ending," the bride and groom encountered Mother Crewe outside the door.

She accused the two of murdering her daughter. A crowd gathered round drawn by the loud shrieking and lamenting of this grieving soul. Elizabeth Crewe began to curse the couple. Molly fell to her knees, pleading with her not to do so, but Mother Crewe railed,

"May your husband fail in all he undertakes and die of a broken heart, and may all your sons be cripples and all your girls abandoned and deserted as mine has been and no one to pity or help them…"

The judge stopped the witch from further curses. The Howlands and Winslows, as well as others on North Street, came out of their homes to see what was going on. Consider Howland was overheard telling his wife, "I will be sure no child of ours will have anything to do with that cursed couple and their offspring."

The judge dispersed the crowd sending a shaken Molly and Ansel on their way. Meanwhile, Elizabeth Crewe somewhat avenged, hobbled through a nearby alleyway, climbed the stairs to Burial Hill, and disappeared.

Chapter 3 – The First of the Curses Come True

Eighteen years passed, but the thought of the curse was never forgotten by the couple or the community. Molly and Ansel struggled, as young couples do, to raise a family and make a living. At first, Ansel found seaman work at the bustling port of Plymouth, but seafaring men are very superstitious, and eventually word spread that Ansel was a cursed man, 'a Jonah', a bad omen to all on board any ship he was assigned. When any mishap occurred on board ship, as it often did, it was blamed on Ansel and the curse of Mother Crewe. Because of this, work became difficult, almost impossible to find. With little or no money, the Rings moved into a hovel on Carver Road.

The Rings were parents to four children, with a fifth on the way. The oldest was named Jack, next came a girl Acsah, a younger daughter named Yetmercy, and a young boy Ichabod.

One March day in the mid-1700s, Ansel Ring was aboard the ship Petrol. The Hedge family in Plymouth owned the coastal schooner. As it returned from Boston, it was caught in a northeast gale, just off the Gurnet Point. The captain decided to ride out the storm. He lay anchor off Dick's Flat to wait for the storm to subside and the tide to change.

The sailors were getting restless. They began proclaiming that the storm was the work of Mother Crewe, and Ansel was to blame. They rumored that unless Ansel was off the ship, all their lives were in danger. Ansel approached the captain and begged for the use of his lifeboat.

"You are a fool to venture out in the storm, Ansel," the captain cried.

"I'd rather take my chances in the small craft, sir than risk my life with this angry mob. If the storm does not subside and our anchor drags, they will toss me overboard. They call me "Jonah," replied Ansel.

So the captain, warning again that no man could survive this angry sea, begged him to try to stick it out a few more hours. When he gazed into the desperate face of this haunted man, he reluctantly ordered the lifeboat lowered.

As Ansel rowed toward Beach Point, his shipmates gathered on deck to watch the spectacle. The dinghy tossed in the monstrous waves, back and forth, up and down, finally crashing against Beach Point.

In the roaring thunderous surf, the seamen had strained to hear his cries, but either Ansel rode to a silent death or the storm muffled his voice.

Ansel's body was thrown on the beach like a ragdoll along with the shattered wreckage.

When the seas subsided, the Petrol glided into Plymouth Harbor. The seamen silently rowed to Beach Point and carried the body of their "Jonah" back into town and down Carver Road home to his awaiting family.

On the threshold of the Ring home stood Mother Crewe. No one knew how she had been first to hear the news, but she had hastened to bring the evil tidings to Molly.

In the midst of the sad lamentations of family and neighbors, and even a bit of remorse on the part of the sailors, Mother Crewe was seen slinking away down a wooded path, with strains of a chuckle and a look of evil pleasure.

Chapter 4 – Ichabod's Tragedy

Six months had passed since the death of their father, and the Ring children had settled into their shabby existence on Carver Road. Molly sent Yetmercy and her little brother into town on an errand. Molly was now eight months pregnant with a fifth child, and not a day went by that she did not weep over the death of Ansel, and worry about how to support her brood.

Yetmercy, now a teenager, sang a tune as they walked along pathways into town, enjoying the crisp, fall day. Ichabod complained that the trip to town tired his feet with his ill-fitting worn-out shoes, but Yetmercy gently admonished him not to complain, and do all he could to help his mother.

A horse and carriage stood parked on School Street. Its owner had stopped in a neighboring shop on an errand. Local boys were up to mischief, as they played a prank on the horse, placing a burr under its tail. The horse restlessly stamped its hooves, and suddenly reared, taking off at a gallop. The boys made an attempt to stop the carriage, but to no avail. Each time the horse flicked its tail, the burr dug deeper, causing him to madden and quicken his pace. The horse and riderless carriage dashed out of control down School Street, rounded the corner into Town Square, and proceeded to Leyden Street just as Yetmercy and little Ichabod stepped into the crossroads.

The sound of the clatter alerted them. They attempted to retreat, but too late. The horse, seeing the young lad, tried to swerve around him, faltered, fell, and the carriage toppled on top of Ichabod. The horse's hooves flailed in every direction, threatening all who tried to come to the boy's rescue.

Yetmercy was screaming and wailing uncontrollably. "Cut the horse loose," someone in the gathering crowd shouted. As a brave soul did so, others were able to step forward and right the wagon.

This took place near Dr. Lazarus Le Baron's office, and he stepped out to examine the commotion. To everyone's relief, he took command of the tragic scene.

Little Ichabod was carried into the doctor's home and laid on a couch to be examined. Yetmercy followed, still wailing and sobbing. Dr. Le Baron's son Isaac, a young intern studying under his father's care, also examined the child.

"Father, I believe the boy has a broken hip and great damage to his spine as well. This is very serious."

"You are right, son," the doctor whispered back, out of hearing of Yetmercy. "This lad will never leave his bed again until he's carried from it to Burial Hill."

With a stern expression Dr. LeBaron turned to Yetmercy, "Young lady, if you care about your mother and your brother you must pull yourself together and be of some assistance now."

"Yes, sir," she weakly replied, trying to control her sobs.

"You had better go on home and have a bed ready downstairs, and get your mother somewhat prepared before we get there."

Young Dr. Isaac was torn at the sad plight of such a lovely, young maid. To lose a father, and now deal with this tragedy, seemed so unfair. He watched as she bravely picked herself up off the floor, brushed back her golden curly locks, wiped her tears, and began the long trek home.

When she returned home, she was shocked to find Elizabeth Crewe sitting on her doorstep. The woman's hunched posture, cavernous eyes, and bitter expression frightened the child. Mother Crewe stepped aside as Yetmercy entered the house.

Shortly after the sad procession approached the hovel on Carver Road, the witch's voice could be heard:

"Molly, Molly Peach! Come out and welcome your child. The foundations of the cursed city were laid in the blood of the firstborn and the posts were set up in the bones of the youngest, and so it shall be, and so it is with you!"

Isaac LeBaron, leading this procession, could not hear or understand Mother Crewe's words, but could read her intent, and observed the look of horror on Yetmercy's face. He sprang forth to her defense.

"What a wicked woman you are! Hold your tongue!" young Dr. LeBaron shouted.

"Have a care, Master Isaac! Have a care! Touch me with just the point of the finger, and I'll wither your arm to the shoulder! "

Isaac shrank back. Her look struck through his blood like a blast from an iceberg. Mother Crewe continued,

"She has blue eyes and pink cheeks, and so had her mother before her, but she is under the curse, and it's catching, catching as small pox. Have a care, Isaac LeBaron Have a care!"

~ 16 ~

With those words, she swiftly departed into the woods, her cackling and chilling laughter drifting back toward the stunned crowd.

Inside the poor cottage, Molly had collapsed and was wailing in grief. After the lifeless form of Ichabod had been settled onto his cot and the crowd dispersed, the doctors left Yetmercy and her siblings with instructions on the care of their injured brother.

The trials of the day were not yet over, for in the middle of the night, Yetmercy pounded on the LeBaron door, frantically looking for their assistance again. Isaac returned to her home to find that Molly had delivered a stillborn child (the last of Ansel Ring's doomed children), and the mother was in danger of dying herself. After many visits in the days to follow, Dr. LeBaron pronounced her very weak and needing much care.

Isaac Le Baron's visits were about the only source of joy for Yetmercy who was now saddled with the care of an ailing mother and an invalid brother. When the doctor would complete his visit, he would linger and steal a moment with Yetmercy and attempt to cheer her. It seemed that a flicker of romance was blossoming.

Chapter 5-Send Her to the Pest House

One day a coastal schooner one of many, darting in and out of Plymouth Harbor, dropped off a sick sailor named John White. Dr. Lazarus LeBaron was called to tend to him. The doctor immediately recognized the dreaded smallpox and informed the town selectmen. A quarantine hut was set up in the outskirts of town called "The Obery".

The town fathers offered great wages to anyone who could undertake the care of this unfortunate man. To everyone's surprise, Mother Crewe came forward as the only volunteer. She explained that she had a bad case of smallpox as a child and lived. She reminded them of the nursing care she had given to her own sick child. With no other candidates for the position, the town granted Elizabeth Crewe the job.

The next day Doctor Isaac LeBaron, son of Lazarus, was sent to check on Mother Crewe and the sailor. She announced that he was doing very poorly. The doctor gave her a large supply of pain medication and sleeping potions to help with the difficult task ahead. He warned that the dreaded disease was spreading and there would likely be more patients to follow. With that grim forecast, the young handsome doctor galloped in haste toward Carver to tend to another patient. It wasn't long after the doctor left that the sailor died.

Mother Crewe devised a plan. She closed the cabin door and headed into town. As she hobbled down the road, she came to the site of the Ring home and found Yetmercy sitting on the front step.

"Did Master Isaac find you? He wants you to give me some help at the Pest House," Mother Crewe said to Yetmercy.

"The Pest House?" exclaimed Yetmercy, turning quite pale at the thought.

"Oh don't look so shocked," replied Mother Crewe. "Dr. LeBaron said it would give him great pleasure for you to aid him. After all, look at the help he has given to you and your family. Besides, the town will give a great reward to those who helped in this work, and your family surely needs the money."

"No money would tempt me to do such a job, but if the doctor needs me, I'll certainly be there," Yetmercy replied. And so despite the calls from her ailing mother for assistance, Yetmercy headed for the pest house with a look of one deeply in love, willing to face any danger or hardship.

When Mother Crewe returned to the Obery, Yetmercy soon arrived behind her. When Yetmercy saw the sailor she exclaimed,

"Mother Crewe, this man is dead."

"Oh no dear, he's just having one of his weak spells. Just rub his hands between your own and his arms and you'll see him come back to life."

"Mother, he frightens me. He is still and cold and has terrible sores."

"Darling," the old woman replied, "and you want to be a doctor's wife? Come dear, comb his hair and make him decent before the doctor arrives."

"But he's dead! I know he's dead, and I'm afraid," shrieked Yetmercy.

"Well now love, perhaps you are right. As a future doctor's wife you might just know these things," crooned the witch." "Then we must get him ready for burial. Come, just get a washcloth and wash his face and see if you can close those glazed staring eyes."

"Oh, I can't! I can't bear it!" shouted Yetmercy. "Let me get out of this place! I need to get out of here!"

In terror, Yetmercy bolted for the door, but Mother Crewe blocked her exit and stood fast, laughing a loud demonic laugh.

"Would you go before your sweetheart comes? Would you let him down this way? Come dear, calm down."

Yetmercy fell to the floor sobbing, and realized for the first time that this was a plot of Mother Crewe's. She fainted on the floor, and when she awoke she was lying in a cot covered with a blanket – the same that covered the body of the now dead sailor. Again she fainted, but not before hearing Elizabeth Crewe crying out to the heavens,

" *Bathsheba's life against hers. My own girl lay like this and none pitied her. Life for a life –*"

Mother Crewe closed the door of the hut, locked it, and set off to town. When she found the selectmen, she reported that her patient was dead, and that she had left Yetmercy to guard the place until proper burial could take place. The evil woman explained that despite her protests, Yetmercy had begged to stay and help.

In alarm, the selectmen asked, "Isn't Yetmercy in danger, since she has not yet had smallpox?"

"Well, perhaps," replied Mother Crewe. " Yetmercy claims she is in love with Isaac LeBaron, and is in desperate need of finances for the family. She thinks no danger can come when she is in his care, and I could not persuade her otherwise."

The town fathers instructed her to roll the dead sailor in tarred sheets, and they would send a grave digger out to bury him.

Mother Crewe was at the door when the grave digger arrived. She warned him not to enter the hut and expose himself to the dreaded disease.

Having tarred and wrapped the body as instructed, she brought it out from the hut herself. So the worker never saw Yetmercy still wrapped in the soiled blanket, and drugged by the medicine that had been left earlier for the sick and dying sailor.

Yetmercy was now in quarantine. Because she had been exposed to small pox, Mother Crewe declared that the distraught girl was obligated to stay in the Pest House until it was proven she would not spread the deadly infection to others in town.

Each time she went into town for supplies, the witch lied, "That foolish girl exposed herself to small pox, but so far, no sign of the disease is with her. She should be released from quarantine soon and be sent home."

When Dr. LeBaron came back to check, Mother Crewe insisted she had desperately tried to turn Yetmercy away, but could not persuade her to leave. She assured the young doctor that soon the girl would be cleared to return to the town and her family.

"In fact," she added, "staying in the Obery has given Yetmercy a chance to catch up on her rest. You know how difficult it has been for her to have taken on all the responsibility of caring for her family. You shouldn't disturb her."

Opening the door as the doctor peered in, he saw the beautiful young girl tucked in with a fresh, clean blanket and sleeping peacefully on the little cot with her blond hair stretched out in curls over her pillow. Reluctantly, Dr. LeBaron left, conflicted by this turn of events. He did not want that dear girl to stay with this evil woman, but he could not argue that she needed to be in quarantine for at least a few more weeks.

But a short time later, Yetmercy did show the telltale signs of small pox and could not leave the Obery. Each time the doctor stopped by, she was asleep. However, before long Yetmercy became the second declared death resulting from the dreaded disease just as Mother Crewe had anticipated.

After notifying officials again, the grave digger returned to bury the wrapped and tarred body in a small field outside of town. Sadly, no one from the Ring family was allowed to attend. The news of the loss of her youngest daughter was more than Molly could bear.

A few days after Yetmercy's burial, Jack Ring, the oldest remaining child, was planning his mother's funeral as well.

Mother Crewe once more collected her payment of silver. She seemed compassionate and generous as she announced to anyone who would listen that she would drop half of the earnings off to the poor remaining Ring children. But as Mother Crewe journeyed back home to her farm in Plympton, neighbors were chilled by the witch's laughter resounding in the surrounding woods.

Chapter 6 – A Day of Horror

As Dr. Lazarus LeBaron rode to Plymouth from Marshfield, wondering what his wife was preparing for his evening meal, he came upon a woman running down a wooded path screaming, shrieking, and wailing. As he approached the hysterical woman, he recognized her as the maidservant of Ichabod English.

In the clearing on a hill overlooking the Jones River sat a cottage. It was the home of Ichabod English, his bride Acsah, and their four children: Molly, Nettie, Dorcas, and a newborn baby. Acsah was the last female child of the Ring family. Acsah and her brother Jack had experienced the loss of their father Ansel, their mother Molly, her stillborn child, Yetmercy, and little Ichabod. Now only Acsah and Jack were left.

Acsah had been left destitute and worn from the series of family tragedies, but her luck had changed when she met a handsome, young sailor who called Plymouth his port. They fell in love and married. Many in the town whispered that Mother Crewe's curse must be worn out, and now at least one of Molly's children was to prosper and be happy.

But this was not to be. As years passed, Ichabod English moved from job to job. He never seemed satisfied. Depression set in, and he constantly worried about his family and its future. Acsah was a loving wife and tried her best to be a good mother and good wife, but she worried about her husband, his restlessness, and erratic behavior.

One day, Ichabod sent his wife and baby off to visit her aunt. He sent the manservant to town to spend the day at the Jenney Grist Mill to get sacks of corn ground for the family. He told the maid, Hannah Crombie, that she could have the day off since he planned an outing with the children while his wife was away.

Dr. LeBaron approached the home. Outside a dog was howling, and a cat paced back and forth with bristling fur. From the hysterical woman and the behavior of the animals, the doctor knew something inside was very wrong.

He passed through a kitchen, eerie and still, then through the parlor calling out to Ichabod and Acsah, and finally came to the bedroom. The setting sun streamed into the room and fooled the doctor for what he was about to discover.

.

On the bed lay Acsah, with the baby on her bosom. Both lay still in death. The only telltale sign that mother and baby were not napping was a crimson red spot on a white sheet. On the floor, next to the bed, were the bodies of the three precious youths. Each was in their night clothes, laid out with their hands across their chests. Each had bloodstained clothing, yet a look of peaceful innocence on their faces. Across the room at a desk, slumped face down, was the form of Ichabod, with a pistol tightly gripped in his hand.

The doctor's heart pounded as he approached the corpse of the man. By his head was a bloodstained dagger in an upright position, piercing the wood of the desk. Under the dagger, shockingly, was a letter addressed to the doctor himself.

Dear Doctor LeBaron,

It seems to me that you will be the first person of responsibility and authority called to witness the work I need to accomplish here today, and while I suspect you will condemn my actions, I believe God will approve.

You know, as do the fathers of Plymouth, that I have come here to your town to earn an honest livelihood and to live a decent life. Yet, you must also know that there are those who come into this world under a curse, and no matter how they strive they cannot be delivered from it.

For many days now I have been confused by the incessant clap of the wings of birds inside my head.

My little children and their mother are of the elect, but I am a reprobate and lost. My money is spent, my debts are pressing, the day of hope is passed, and I can work no more, for the birds blind my eyes and my brain with the whirling of their wings.

I have a right to my own life, and I will take it.

I hold myself responsible for the lives of these children, and I will not leave them to starvation and the cruel, cruel world. I shall take them with me, my brave boy and my pretty little maids. But I have no rights to the life of Acsah, and I determined that she should have her baby to console her. The little nursing baby can comfort her.

So I saw Acsah was heavy hearted and sent her to see the "granddame" as Acsah fondly calls her aunt. When she left I sent the manservant to town knowing his errand would take all day. I told the maid she should take the day off and spend it with her people that I planned to go away with the children. (It made me laugh in my head to think how I told her no lie, for indeed I would go away and take the children. No lie, for I am an honorable man, yes and a good father!)

Wait, what is that noise?

The letter broke off abruptly, with a blot as if the pen had fallen, then began again.

~ 28 ~

She has come back with the baby. She said she was almost at granddame's when something, she knew not what, came over her and forced her to turn back. She was crying and asked why I looked so strange. She asked why I had dressed the children in the night clothes when it was still day.

Suddenly the sky darkened and the storm arose. And with the wind came the voices.

I will take her first so she will not see the little ones die. I will make it also gentle and tender, for I have been a good husband and father. And I would have been a good man if not born predestined.

Well, I will not delay, let me but sign my name, for I never did work I was ashamed to set my name to. I am an honest and honorable man.

Ichabod English

Did the family know what was about to happen? The tragedy appeared to be completed without terror to the victims. Possibly, Acsah and the children may have been drugged first. Opium was found in the house, and it was suspected that English was a victim of its abuse.

So ended the life of another offspring of Ansel and Molly Ring, as the curses of Mother Crewe continued to unfold.

Chapter 7 – The Last of the Rings

The first of May brought the fragrant blossoms of the Mayflower bush (trailing arbutus) and with it a tradition of love and romance. It seems in Plymouth (somewhat like Valentine's Day) that a young man could pick a cluster of Mayflowers, and call on a young lady. If he arrived first at her door, presenting her with this romantic bouquet, it was a sign of his affection, and one she could not easily refuse.

Well, Hannah Howland and Priscilla Le Baron devised a plot of their own to stave off the unwanted affections of certain young suitors. They planned to get up at the crack of dawn, gather their own bouquet of flowers, and be ready to stand by their doors to announce, "Oh, I'm sorry you took the trouble, but you're too late. I have some already."

At the first light, Priscilla and Hannah headed out with baskets in hand for a grand adventure. They arrived at the Billington Sea*, and sat to eat some bread, and quench their thirst with the fresh spring water. Realizing their baskets still were not full, they continued on.

*Note: Billington Sea is a 269-acre warm water pond located in Plymouth. According to legends it was named after Frances Billington who climbed a tree and saw water on the horizon. He believed he was looking at the Pacific Ocean, and the pond received its name by the Pilgrims as a result. It still bears that same name today.

Following chirping birds down a slippery slope, Hannah spotted a spray of Mayflowers. She started to leap across a small stream, when a noise in the brush startled her. She sprang sideways, tripping in a bog hole.

"Oh, I hope you'll forgive me for startling you, Miss Howland."

"Oh my foot!" she exclaimed, and stumbled forward, landing in the strong arms of a young man. "My ankle is sprained, maybe broken," she moaned.

Suddenly, Priscilla arrived out of breath, surprised to find her friend in the arms of a total stranger.

"Can you walk at all dear?" Priscilla asked in a tone that seemed somewhat indignant. She was feeling quite unsettled at the sight of her best friend in a position no Plymouth maiden would consider proper.

"No," the man quickly responded. "If she could stand, she would not allow me to …hold the bushes aside, and I will bring her up the banking." The stranger lifted Hannah's slight form, carried her up the steep hill, and tenderly set her on a log. "Now if you will sit beside her, I'll go to the village for help."

"I can go quicker," replied Priscilla, "I know just where to get help."

All agreed, and as Priscilla dashed down the wooded path, Hannah realized they were alone.

She timidly asked, "You are a stranger here, are you not? You called me Miss Howland. How could you possibly know my name?" She was looking quite flushed and confused.

"I am a sailor on board Capt. Samson's brig, The Lydia," he replied.

"Oh, my family knows Capt. Samson well. In fact, he dined at our home last night," Hannah replied, with a sigh of relief at the connection. "What is your name?"

"They call me Jack," he responded, with a slight hesitation.

"What is your family name?" Hannah pressed further.

"Oh, we poor sailors do not use family names," he replied. "But I know you are Miss Howland. I have seen you often in Plymouth, but you have not noticed me. I was here in the woods to gather Mayflowers. Let me show you." Jack dashed down a hill and returned with a basket of beautiful flowers fresh with dew.

"Oh, how beautiful they are. Finer than any we have picked ourselves today," Hannah "Yes, I was picking these for you," he confessed with a blush.

"For ME?"

"Yes, I sent you some last year."

"Those were from you? But who are you?"

"Yes, I did. Whenever I sail around the world I hope to be back here in Plymouth to pick the first May flowers for you every year until…"

"Until when, Jack?"

"Until you marry."

"Oh, that may never be."

The conversation was interrupted by the sounds of the wagon. The servant Quasho and Capt. Samson arrived announcing that Priscilla stayed behind at the Le Baron home waiting for their return.

"You here Ring!" exclaimed the captain.

"Yes, sir. I was lucky enough to be near when Miss Howland hurt herself."

"Ring!" exclaimed Hannah.

"Yes," the sailor admitted bitterly. "I'm the only one left alive from the Ring family that Mother Crewe cursed.

I was named Ansel after my father, but I just go by the name Jack."

"Well, it doesn't matter to this young girl," exclaimed the captain, "and I haven't told the men your last name."

"Goodbye, Miss Howland," Jack Ring softly said. He picked up the basket of Mayflowers, handed it to Hannah, lifting her carefully onto the wagon, and disappeared into the woods.

Chapter 8 – Tragedy Strikes Again

Months had passed since Hannah and Jack first met. Each time his ship came to port, Hannah managed to be down by the wharves. Their secret meetings grew in number until Jack promised he would earn enough to take her away as his bride.

Hannah knew her family would never bless their marriage. She had grown up listening to her father tell tales about Mother Crewe and the curse of the Rings. Everyone in town had shunned the family, but Hannah's mother and father were dead. Her brother, Thomas Southworth was the head of the house, but there was not much love between her and her land hungry, power-hungry sibling.

Hannah had secretly decided to trust her future with that handsome sailor, Jack. Yet, in the depths of her soul, she felt fear and a sense of gloom that she could not shake.

It was Christmas Eve, 1778, and while part of the world was celebrating the holiday, most folks in Plymouth had not even heard of Christmas. They saw it as "a Papist Holiday", something of that scorned Catholic tradition, something certainly not to revere.

As Hannah sat at home, wondering when Jack might return, she noticed that a storm was brewing, and the winds were howling. Before long, the entire town was a-stir with the news of a terrible shipwreck in Plymouth Harbor. For three days the storm raged, and Hannah's fears were for her sailor, Jack. Could he be on that ship? Was he on another ship out there on the raging sea?

Victims of the tragedy at sea were laid out first in the Town Brook, to thaw the frozen bodies, then later in the Town House, for possible identification. Residents opened their doors to the few survivors. The ship's captain, James McGee, was hosted at the Howland house.

When the worn captain was alone, sitting by the hearth, Hannah stole into the room and whispered, "Captain McGee, I am Mr. Howland's sister, and I wish to ask you a question. Did a man named Ansel or Jack Ring sail among your ship's crew?"

"No, I do not remember such a name. But honestly Miss, we had just left port. I could not possibly know the names of all my men. Do you think he was on board my ship, The General Arnold?"

"I'm not sure of the name of the ship. I am so afraid he was. I must go to Town Hall and see."

"No, no,my dear. It is no sight for a young lady such as you," the captain warned.

"Thank you, sir, for your advice," Hannah replied, knowing she would not heed his warning, but must see for herself.

The next day funeral services were held in the Town Hall (now the 1749 Court House) for 60 of the unknown men. When Rev. Robbins entered the building, he fainted at the grotesque site. All the men in town were there, and a few hardy women. One woman was heavily veiled, and not recognized. She moved from body to body looking with unflinching eyes at a sight most strong men could not bear. She stopped beside a form identified by no one else. It was the body of Ansel Ring.

The last of the Rings, Jack was laid to rest in a mass grave on Burial Hill.

Hannah never recovered from that day. Not long after, she confided to her best friend Lydia that it had been Jack's body she observed. She could not forgive herself for not publicly identifying his body and allowing him to have a proper burial, even knowing she would have been shunned by neighbors and incurred the wrath of her brother. Wracked with grief, she was frequently seen climbing Burial Hill. Town folks surmised she was paying respects to her family and relatives long deceased. Yet when no one else was nearby, she would pass the Howland graves and continue on the hill to the mass grave of those poor souls buried there, including her true love, Jack Ring.

When she told Lydia she knew that, like Jack, she was under the curse of Mother Crewe and her future was doomed, Lydia exclaimed,

"Hannah, no! That is not true. You mustn't believe this. You will be fine. Just give yourself time!"

As time went on, however, Hannah grew thinner and weaker. As Lydia became a frequent visitor to the Howland home, to check on her ailing friend, Hannah once confided more to her. Hannah recalled an occasion a year before the tragedy she had stolen away with Jack while he had been in port. As they strolled the wooden paths by the Plympton Road secretly making wedding plans, they had the unfortunate chance to cross paths with Mother Crewe. She surprised them and left muttering and cackling to herself.

"I saw her," Hannah exclaimed to Lydia. "She gave me the evil eye and muttered curses to us under her breath. I know there is no hope for me as there was none for my love, Jack, and because I love him, I too am cursed."

On Christmas of 1779, Hannah took to bed, reliving the anniversary of the tragic shipwreck. On January 25, 1780, she died. The doctor, unable to find a specific illness, declared she died of a "languishment."

Lydia never disclosed the secret her best friend Hannah carried to her grave.

Inscription on Hannah Howland's Grave on Burial Hill, Plymouth, Massachusetts:

"To the memory of Miss Hannah Howland who died of a languishment January ye 25th 1780 Etaitis 26
For us they languish & for us they die And shall they languish shall they die in vain."

: Photo Diane Finn- Burial Hill Hannah Howland's Grave

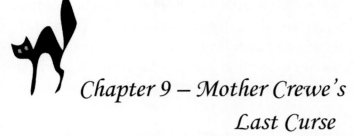 *Chapter 9 – Mother Crewe's Last Curse*

Thomas Southworth Howland was surveying his land. He loved the feeling of power that came with land ownership. As the Revolution was drawing to a close, it was important to consolidate his land titles, in case they came into question. One such piece was a 10-acre plot in West Plymouth, by the Carver Road.

One day he rode out to view it and arranged for it to be staked out and fenced. The land was as he expected to find, but right in the center stood a tiny, dilapidated shed. As he approached the cabin, a thin column of smoke trailed from its meager chimney.

"Who is trespassing on my property?" he shouted angrily. He rode his horse to the cabin door and beat on it with his whip. The door flew open, and on the threshold appeared the bent figure of Mother Crewe, with her cat Milicom perched on her shoulder and a staff in her hand.

"Well, man of violence and wrath, what do you want here?" Mother Crewe asked in a grating voice.

"What do I want?" he shouted. "I think the question is what you are doing on another man's property. This land is mine and I intend to fence it and cultivate it. I don't want a tenant on it, and you will have to vacate at once. This week a plow will be running over the very spot on which you stand. Do you understand, Mother Crewe?"

Mother Crewe's voice rose as she spoke.

> *"This week, this week man of violence and wrath they will dig your grave on Burial Hill. I see it. I hear it. I smell the fresh earth they throw out. Go home and make your peace, and set your house in order."*

Thomas Southworth could feel his blood begin to boil in rage as he responded with blasphemous oaths, warning her that before the next day's sunset his land would be rid of her, and her hovel would be leveled in the dust. He added that if she could be found she would be burned at the stake as a witch.

Mother Crewe raised a skinny finger toward him in reply,

> *"Carry him home the gate will do. Come wife, sister, children, scream. Cover your eyes. Die poor maid, broken by the curse on Ansel Ring, killed by the curse on Southworth Howland. Die poor maid for the sins of others."*(Here she is referring to Hannah Howland)

~ 42 ~

As if Thomas's horse was frightened by her rage, the horse began to stir nervously. Thomas pulled back his stallion, and Mother Crewe disappeared into the hut. Howland rode back to town shouting warning that he would have a legal eviction notice, and return in the morning with the sheriff.

The next day, just before noon, a small band of townsfolk including the Sheriff and his squire, and Thomas Howland ventured out to the Howland property with an eviction notice in hand. Arriving at the clearing, they hoped to see some sign of surrender or vacancy, but the smoke curled upward, and the door was shut. Nothing had been moved.

Howland galloped to the door and again struck it with his whip handle. The door opened and Mother Crewe, with Milicom on her shoulder, appeared.

"Well woman," he shouted, "you have had your warning, and you are not gone."

"My warning! It is your warning that is in the air man, and you will soon be gone," croaked Mother Crewe.

Thomas Southworth Howland began to shake with rage, and shouted, "Here, we'll end it all! Men, pull the cabin down around the old witch's ears. You've got your warrant for it! Now do it!"

Seated high upon his horse, he kicked his heels into the shuttered window and smashed it. The men silently obeyed and began to whirl their axes into the shabby dwelling.

"Wait! Hold your handles hirelings while I speak to your master," railed the old woman. "Man of violence, you have been warned yet you persist. I am an old woman. I bothered no one. I have lived here for many years. You own all this land. What is one small parcel against all your holdings? If you continue your wrath of violence against me, you are rushing your own destruction. Just say one word of kindness. Speak before it's too late."

Howland responded with, "Set fire to her place. Burn it to the ground! Burn the witch and her house together."

"Enough," shouted Mother Crewe.
"Man I curse you living. I curse you dying. I curse you here. I curse you hereafter."

Was it the woman or was it the cat? None could tell, but in the midst of the curses and shouting Milicom sprang from his mistresses' shoulder to the flank of Howland's horse. The horse reared and took off at an uncontrollable gallop darting down the wood path out of sight.

Thomas Southworth's friends and Sheriff followed as fast as they could, but at a sharp turn they came upon Thomas' body lying in the scrub oak. He had hit his head on a tree limb and died. The horse had galloped away. Friends spied an old fence with a gate nearby. Laying his body on the gate (just as Mother Crewe had predicted) in solemn procession, Thomas Southworth Howland was brought back into town and later buried on Burial Hill.

As the lifeless body passed by, Mother Crewe muttered,

> *"It had to be man, it had to be, and we shall meet very soon. What has to be will be, for me as well as for you."*

The old woman and her cat disappeared into the woods.

Chapter 10 – The End Has Come

Weeks after the death of Thomas Howland, there was a strange yellow light and murky glow in the air. The sun was veiled by a smoky glare of amber light. To the west, low reddish clouds hung like tarnished copper.

The color of the sky and sea frightened the folks in Plymouth. Some whispered that the end of the world was at hand. Some fell to their knees and prayed. Others thought about their debts and unfinished business, and began to repay their neighbors and confess their sins.

The next morning showed some improvement and relief, and farmers went about their business, bringing in the hay and feeding their animals.

Farmer Butler was out in his fields when his five-year-old son Ruben ran toward him. Laughingly, he threw the boy on top of the wagon in the hay and, they began to joke and play. Dark clouds rolled in from the west, and the sky turned a strange yellow color. Rumbles of thunder were heard in the distance. Farmer Butler knew he had to hurry to secure his animals. He bade his son to run home to his mother before the storm broke. The small child giggled and ran barefoot over the hill toward the farmhouse.

Darkness swept in with an unexpected suddenness, and as the blackened, ash-filled rains fell, Farmer Butler ran home. In the yard, his wife greeted him.

"Have you got Ruben?" she inquired. "Goodness, you face is black."

"Our son? Isn't he here with you?" cried the farmer, as he wiped the soot off his face. The pelting rain and dark, dark sky drove the woman back into the house. Her husband unyoked the oxen and steered them into the barn. As he made his way back to the farmhouse, the sheets of rain and lack of light left him groping like a blind man.

Meanwhile, the little boy had wandered toward a raspberry patch and was enjoying the fruit when the sky darkened even more, and a loud clap of thunder and stream of rain startled him. Running in the wrong direction, he headed away from the safety of his home, and ran like a frightened rabbit for many miles in the terror of the strange storm.

He ran right through the town past the home of the Howland's, where Thomas had been laid out on the table, while his wife wept uncontrollably, and sister Hannah took to her bed, devastated by the horrible death of her lover, followed by her brother's demise.

By nightfall, Rubin was worn out from his cries for mommy and daddy, and his long trek on a strange road.

A voice called out, "Come here, lad," and in exhaustion, he collapsed in an old lady's arms.

That night, a frantic couple, Mr. and Mrs. Butler arrived at Parson Leonard's door on Leyden Street, telling of the lost child. A search party was quickly formed. One old gentleman talked of seeing a young lad along the Plympton Road.

The search party spent that night and the next day combing the Plympton Road and surrounding wooded areas. They were about to give up at dusk, but the trusty pet of the young boy barked furiously, and the child's mother begged them to follow. The dog led them to a stone wall and a graveyard by a church in Plympton, and there under a heap of a black cloak was the frightened, whimpering child. As the thick, black cloak was lifted, the remains of a haggard old woman appeared.

"Did this lady kidnap you?" snapped one of the search party.

"No," exclaimed the child, now in the arms of his tearful mother smothering his berry-stained face with kisses. "This nice lady kept me warm and dry. She fed me berries gave me water to drink," the lad cheerfully explained.

There at the base of the old stone wall lay the corpse of the old woman, Elizabeth Crewe.

"Dear Lord, this is Mother Crewe," shouted one of the search party.

"She is a witch! Throw her body to the wolves," shouted another.

"Oh no, stop this talk," said Mrs. Butler. "This woman saved my child's life. Look, she has come to rest by this stone wall near to her daughter's grave. She deserves a proper burial next to Bathsheba, her only child."

And so the woman was obeyed, and in her death Mother Crewe was more honored than in her life.

The day that many thought of as "The End of the World" marked the end of the life and curses of Mother Crewe.

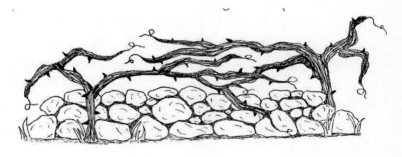

Notes from the author:

If you take a trip to historic Plymouth Center, you will find many landmarks mentioned in this story. On Burial Hill, you can locate the graves of Thomas Southworth Howland and Hannah Howland, and the graves of the LeBaron family: Dr. Francis, Lazarus, and Isaac. A bit further back is the memorial to the sailors who died in the wreck of the General Arnold.

Descend the stairs toward the waterfront and you'll find the 1749 Court House, formerly the Town House, and the site where the bodies were laid for identification. Stroll along Leyden Street and look to a home on the south side with a plaque to mark the site of Pastor Leonard's home. A bit further on is LeBaron Alley, named after that famous family of physicians. To the right is the Town Brook and picturesque Brewster Garden, where those frozen sailors were laid out to be thawed and their limbs straightened for burial.

Heading north toward North Street (called Queen Street until after the Revolution) you'll see the Captain Randall mansion and at the top of North Street (perhaps by New World Tavern) the home of the Justice of the Peace. Jane Goodwin Austin mentions that during the original curse of Mother Crewe, the Howland and Winslow families came out of their homes to view the spectacle. Research will show that the building where the shop known as the Laughing Moon is located was once called the Howland Block and the building on the opposite side of North Street (now a bakery) was the home of the famous General John Winslow who resided there in the mid-1700s.

Austin sets the death of Mother Crewe as the same day as the "Day of Darkness" (The dates are close but do not exactly coincide with Thomas Southworth's death). Several articles have been written about the date May 19, 1780, called "New England's Dark Day".

In one article by Randy Alfred in 2008, it is explained that in the midst of the Revolutionary War, darkness descended throughout New England, leaving many people to think that Judgment Day was at hand.

An article written by John Horrigan claims many newspapers and journals from that date validate that this event **did** occur. Some New England residents repented their sins and returned stolen and borrowed goods to their neighbors believing the end of the world was at hand.

This strange event came on quickly from the west, and did not end until the following day. A strange copper-colored hue blanketed the sky from sunset to sunrise.

One description explains that at 10 AM the skies darkened, that crickets began chirping and cows returned to their stalls. Farmers, schoolboys, and fishermen could not understand why the sun was missing. The noonday meal had to be served by candlelight, and one could scarcely read the print from local newspapers.

A reporter in Massachusetts said it began to shower and looked as though a powerful storm was approaching from the southwest. While the sky churned and boiled at high altitudes, the blades of grass were not stirring at the ground level. By 3 PM there was perceived a strong sooty smell and nothing but black ash fell from the sky. Many birds were found dead on the ground followed by a thick smoke, but by the next morning things were back to normal and the sun returned.

The dark day seemed to be over. Most documentation agrees that massive wildfires in the west during the spring of 1780 were the likely source of this infamous day.

Bethia Hazel's Revenge

By Diane Finn
Adapted from: David Alden's Daughter and Other Stories of
Colonial Times by Jane Goodwin Austin

Chapter 1-The Entail

Captain Thomas Randall stood on the crest of Burial Hill with his son Philip. They were gazing at the new tombstone that had just been erected for Philip's grandfather, Gregory, in his freshly dug grave.

Much to the surprise of Philip, Thomas seemed to be in very good spirits. Philip could not understand why, because the sudden death of his grandfather had been a very sad occasion for the Randall family.

Looking down at the beautiful view from the crest of Burial Hill on this sparkling spring morning, Thomas marveled at the sweeping sight of Plymouth Harbor, Duxbury, Standish homestead, the Gurnet with its twin lighthouses, and Beach Point with its white dunes and glittering sand. He turned to Philip and proclaimed with great excitement,

"I have some amazing news to tell you. I have been organizing and scouring your grandfather's records through the night and discovered a document referred to as an entail. Do you know what that means? Do you have any idea how important this document is for you, for me, for your children to come?"

"Father, I have not heard of such a thing."

"Son, it seems that King Charles I had bestowed on your great-grandfather, John, a huge plot of land in Plymouth. This plot starts at the shore by the Forefathers Rock and to the Cypress trees by the brook all the way north to the Cold Spring and west to the main road that was once the Indian trail to Sandwich. Philip, this land is priceless! It is our birthright, our families, and all future male heirs in the Randall line. I cannot understand why your grandfather did not share this information with us before."

"But father, "Philip said, somewhat distressed. "Many other people have built their dwellings on this land and claim it for their own. How can we say it is ours?"

Captain Randall smiled, "Entail is a very special document, my son. It will change the course of our lives and the lives of our heirs to come."

"Father, entail indeed! Who ever heard of such a thing in New England? We have no such institutions here."

"We live by English rule, and we govern ourselves by English law, do we not?" replied his father. "What is legal in the parent country must also be legal in the colonies."

"This seems most unjust. People have built their homes, and improved their lands and they suppose it to be their own," Philip argued.

"These poor folk can now become our tenants, or make satisfaction for the trespass they have committed. Why, we'll let them purchase their land at whatever price we and the court determine is fair."

"Father, while we are talking about our future and our heirs, I wish to inform you that I have good news of my own. I am planning to marry, and the name of the young lady is Judith Hazel."

There was a long silence before Captain Randall sputtered,

"Judith Hazel what are you talking about, son? Is she the daughter of the old witch Bethia? That hag should have been burned at stake long ago. Bethia Hazel weaves for a living. She is a penniless wench. She comes from such poor, folk that she and her mother once worked for my parents. Why Bethia cleaned my muddy boots and emptied our chamber pots too!"

"Yes, she is old, poor and widowed," responded Phillip. "As for witchcraft, we are not supposed to believe in such matters here. It's 50 years since the terrible ordeal of the hangings in Salem, and the world has moved on since then."

"Not so fast young man," said Thomas. Changes have occurred but that does not release children from their duty to their parents. As your father, I forbid you to think or speak of this matter further. When you marry, I can promise you it will be to someone much more to your station."

"Father, I am 22 years of age and able to make my own choice."

"Two and twenty fools in one then!" roared his father. "Are you going to defy me, son?"

"I do not intend to, but only bring to mind that I'm a grown man and I can judge for myself. This is a very personal and dear matter to me."

"I suppose you believe you are able to earn your own living. How do you and your lady wife plan to support yourselves?"

"I don't doubt, father, that I can find the means to support myself with whomever I take as my bride."

Captain Randall angrily responded, "You need remember that everything you have, every view you see, everything you've possessed, everything you enjoy the clothes on your back, the food that you eat, they're all my bounty! You are nothing more than a beggar, a dependent, and you have lived off the fruits of my hard work and my industry."

"Well father, now that your estate is entailed...," Philip sneered.

"Son, the entail could be set aside and it shall be. I will claim this property to which you presume to tell me I have no right, and then I will take measures to secure your obedience, or I will turn you and your witch's brat of a wife upon the world with a father's curse for your only inheritance," Thomas raged. "Yes, Philip, a witch's brat for a bride. Once and for all, I forbid you to visit or even speak with her again. I forbid you! Do you understand?"

"I understand, sir."

"And you will obey?"

"Most assuredly I will **not** obey!"

"You will not?"

"I will not obey you in this, so help me God, Father." Philip walked away from his father leaving Captain Randall in pain, anger, disappointment and despair.

As he descended the steep path from Burial Hill, Captain Randall returned to his home on North Street. There, on the second floor of the Randall estate, he spent the rest of the day and long into the night looking through his records, checking maps, determining what he would do next. Finally, he devised a plan for his revenge.

Chapter 2- The Betrothal

As the sun rose over Plymouth Bay, Judith Hazel threw open the shutters to her shabby home. The fresh ocean breeze and the sunlight of a new morning brightened her surroundings and her spirit. To her surprise, Philip was asleep on her front stoop.

As Judith sprung the front door open, she exclaimed, "Philip, what are you doing here? Is something wrong?"

Philip stretched, rubbed his shoulders, and stood up. It had been a long and sleepless night on the stoop, but he was determined to share his love and his intention. Gazing at Judith, he admired the tall and slender girl, her graceful figure despite her homespun dress, the skimpy skirt exposing her bare feet and ankles. Her complexion was clear and glowing. Her hair was dark and wavy, framing eyes brown and bright, her disposition as cheerful as the glow from the rising sun.

"Philip," asked Judith again with concern. "What is the matter? What has happened? Why are you here?"

"Come over here, Judith and walk with me. I have something to tell you." Philip took her hand and led her gently down the path by a meadow to a spring behind her cottage. It was named "Cold Spring" by the First Comers, later known as the Pilgrims. Judith followed, her bare feet treading through the dewy grass strewn with daisies and buttercups.

"Judith, you know that I love you, but I have never asked you to be my wife."

"Stop teasing me, Philip. That is not something to take lightly or joke about. I never expected you would ask, for I'm not fit to be your wife. You know your father would never have me. I do know you love me, and I love you dearly, but our lives together just cannot be." Judith's eyes filled with tears.

As she turned to go, Philip grabbed her shoulders and stopped her. "Judith, I did not come here to tease you or to make you cry. Please hear me out. I stand here alone, without money, position or even knowing how I'm going to gain your respect and my livelihood. My father and I have quarreled, and he has cast me off. Before the sun reaches the top of those trees, I will be gone from Plymouth, gone for many years to make a fortune and become the man that can take you for a wife. Judith, would you have me for your husband, just the way I am?"

Judith wrapped her arms around Philip's neck and laid her head on his chest. He gathered her close to his heart, and as they stood by the brook entangled in each other's arms, smothering each other with tender kisses, they agreed to a secret marriage that very day. The decision was reached that it would be best if they could move in with some of Philip's friends living in Boston, and he could build a career in the city.

After several minutes lost in thought Judith returned to her senses. "Philip, I feel very badly leaving my mother but if it is what must be, then I will do it."

"It must be this way. I ask you for the love of me to come now, and we will be married in Kingston before nightfall."

So Judith crept into the house, filled with excitement for the adventure of her new life that lay ahead. With a pang of guilt about not first sharing this news with her mother, she made her preparations and carefully crept out without disturbing or waking her mother, Bethia.

Judith climbed on the horse behind Philip, and they headed out along the shore road to Kingston to begin their new life. They knew there would be many obstacles ahead, but believed as young lovers all do that their love would conquer all.

Chapter 3- Bethia Hazel Curses Captain Randall

When Bethia Hazel awoke, she searched the home and landscape for her missing daughter. As she examined the horse's hoof prints in the sand, it did not take her long to figure that Judith had been whisked away by Philip Randall. Despite her warning that a friendship with Phillip could lead to disaster, she knew that when a girl is in love she listens to no one, and sense and reason do not come into question.

Suddenly, Bethia heard horses' hooves coming up the path to her humble home. At first, she thought it was her daughter and Phillip returning from a morning country ride, but soon she saw it was three men heading toward her. The central figure was a man 60 years old. She recognized the figure of Thomas Randall, with his commanding and haughty bearing. His eyes looked weary but fierce and angry. His countenance was stern and filled with rage.

The threesome arrived at her doorstep. The sheriff with his assistant leaped from their horses, but Capt. Randall rode close to the doorway where Hazel was standing, and did not dismount.

"Are you here looking for your son Captain Randall?" Bethia asked, in a mocking tone.

"What have you done with my son, Goodwife Hazel? I have come here today to give you a warning."

"Oh really now, sir. You shall get one in return. What warning might that be?"

"I'm giving you a warning to quickly leave these premises," Captain Randall barked.

"Leave these premises?" echoed Bethia. "Why would I want to leave the house where I was born, where I expect to die? Why would I leave except for my concern over my missing daughter, Captain Thomas Randall?"

"Because this property belongs to me. My father and my grandfather allowed you and others to occupy their land, but they never intended you to own it. The land is mine and I no longer choose you should occupy it. Do you understand? I have papers to prove it. I have an entail bestowed upon my grandfather by the King himself. This house you have chosen to put on this land becomes mine also."

"I am, however, a reasonable man, and on condition that you and yours should leave this part of the country, this very town, I will give you whatever we decide is an honest sum. You can come to my office tomorrow and receive the fair money I will pay you. However, if you ever come within my reach or home afterwards, I'll have you thrown in jail for rent and damages, and you can live or rot there until you die."

Bethia remained calm, never moving or changing her position during Thomas' tirade. When he finished, she raised her head, opened her eyes wide, took a deep breath and said,

"Captain Randall, you really mean to turn me out of my house and off my land? I have lived here and so have those before me, for over 100 years. You truly think you can drive me out of this town with a meager price offering? Is that what you think Captain Randall?"

"Yes, I expect you to leave this home within a week, or I will burn it over your head."

"I will not go!"

"If you will not, I'll tell you, witch, you will go if I have to drag you from this place with my own hands, you and that daughter of yours, too."

"My daughter? If my daughter is a problem, whose fault is that but your son's? So I ask *you,* Captain Randall, I ask back my girl, and you shall give her to me or I will have the town about *your* ears. What have you done with my daughter? Where is she and where is your son, Philip?"

~ 65 ~

Captain Randall replied, "He is gone, but I will have my revenge. I will have justice as sure as there is a heaven. You will be burned as a witch, and your wayward daughter will be sent to the stocks, lashed and driven out of the town as a shamed woman. You and your daughter have robbed me of my son, and you shall pay me, even to the last gasp of your breath and last drop of your evil blood. You have defied me, and I will not spare you, as surely as the Heavens above are my witness."

Bethia Hazel took one step forward. Holding his eyes, she took in one deep breath before she spoke,

> "I will not die until you are dead before me. I will not leave my home until you have left yours for the graveyard. I will not leave this town, until you have left this earth. I will not be burned as a witch until you have died like a dog wanting a priest and leach and shelter. You have threatened me, Thomas Randall, and I curse you. I curse you with the black and deadly curse of a widow and the fatherless, and the poor, and the oppressed; I curse you, and so the curse on you descends."

Extending her arm, her bony fingers quivering, she pointed full face at Thomas Randall.

She did so as his look of distress grew and grew, and a deep crimson flush filled his face. Then with one grasping cry, Thomas Randall swayed heavily sideways in the saddle while the attendants raced to stop him. He dropped to the ground at the site of Hazel's very feet.

"He is dead. The curse has fallen upon him," she said, quietly going to her house, shutting and barring the door.

The two men, being more afraid of her than their dead master, mounted their horses and galloped down the hill. There lay Thomas Randall on Bethia Hazel's doorstep, having died like a dog as she had said, without comfort, without shelter from the blazing sun, and without forgiveness.

Half an hour later, the men returned with some townfolk and a wagon. It was only his corpse they carried back to his weeping wife, while his son was nowhere to be found.

Chapter 4 - The Newlyweds' Shocking Discovery

The next morning, Philip and his new bride Judith galloped merrily up the path to the Hazel cottage. The young couple had come to confess to Goodwife Hazel what they had done and bid farewell. They planned to explain to Bethia how generous they intended to be to her after Phillip earned a fortune. Neither of them doubted that this would be so. When they arrived, the door was fastened. Judith went around the backside, but that was fastened also. They shouted long and loud to get Bethia's attention, expecting the door to open at any moment.

Suddenly, they heard a wild shriek from within the house. It was long and shrill, and pierced the quiet summer morning. The newlyweds stood silent, trying to imagine the source of the sound. Judith found an open window, climbed in and unlatched the locked door.

Hand in hand, she and Phillip searched each room, expecting horrible sights. When the rooms had been searched, they climbed the stairs to a loft that had very little light except for single pane glass at the end. Peering into the darkness, they heard a strange laugh overhead.

As they looked up, on a rafter above perched Bethia Hazel. Her gray hair streamed down; her eyes were glazed in madness. Muttering incessantly and laughing she shrieked:

"I cursed him, I cursed him and he fell dead at my feet. Oh, handsome Thomas Randall. When I was a maid in his father's house, I told him I would go to destruction for a kiss of his proud lips, and he laughed at me. He laughed at me! Handsome Thomas Randall, oh, how I loved him and how I hated him! And I cursed him, and he died, there in the hot sun at my doorstep. Not a hand now to brush the flies from his dead face, and even I never cared to kiss him then! I cursed him and he died, and now I must die, and then he will love me, and I shall get my kiss at last."

She had knotted a rope and placed it around her neck. With one last shrill shriek, she leaped forward from the beam. Phillip and Judith rushed forth to stop her. But before they could, the noose had tightened and she was suspended in the air for one horrifying minute. When they could ease her down, amidst Judith's own shrieks and sobs and wails, it was determined that Bethia was unconscious, not dead. As they carried her to her bed below, they made every attempt to revive her, but to no avail.

The attempt was not fatal, but from the shock, Bethia never fully recovered her senses. Judith had run.

to town for assistance from the doctor, and it was there she learned the devastating news about Philip's father

Now it was Judith's turn to console her new husband as he sobbed into her arms at his loss and the bitter words that could not be taken back. "He died without forgiving me, or hearing me tell of my love for him, despite all that we had said to one another."

Chapter 5 - The Ghost of Bethia Hazel

Witch Hazel, as she was thereafter called, spent the rest of her days in her house in the company of a caretaker paid for by Philip. Judith, even with her new duties as a wife and young mother, never failed to make a daily visit to the lonely cottage in which she herself had been born and bred. Eventually, Bethia Hazel died, and her children buried her on a little knoll near her home and land, with the babbling sounds of the Cold Spring, and the sweeping views of Plymouth Bay.

As the years passed, Philip and Judith learned to live with their tragic losses. Their family grew, and their respect in the community also grew as their hard work and dedication were rewarded. The entail was never spoken of again, and life in the Old Colony and the Randall family prospered.

For many years after and sometimes to this very day, people who lived in nearby towns declared that Witch Hazel's ghost could be spotted on any stormy night, wandering between the ruins of her home and Forefather's Rock (now called Plymouth Rock) as she drifts through the cypresses, wringing her hands and wailing above the wind, "I cursed him and he died, he fell dead at my feet. I cursed him and he died he fell dead at my feet. Oh, Captain where are you? I await your kiss."

Note: In Jane Goodwin Austin's book, the witch is "Judith" and the daughter is named "Bethia". For many years we performed this story during Halloween season and told the story of Witch Hazel. The actress (Joyce) liked the old-fashioned name of "Bethia" better for the main character, so I have retold the story here as we shared it with our guests over those many years.

Aunt Rachael's Curse

By Diane Finn
Adapted from: Joseph Chandler Godey's Ladies Magazine
and Charles Skinner, Myths & Legends of Our Own Land

Chapter 1 -The Mooncussers Leave a Widow

Rachael was a fortuneteller best known for her accurate ability to predict the weather. This skill was especially valuable to all the seafaring men on Cape Cod. Many a sailor and sea captain consulted her before venturing out on a long voyage.

Rachael's husband had been a sailor. As a young couple, they had made a fine life together in Eastham in a quaint home along the shores of Cape Cod. This area thrived on the fishing and ship cargo trade, but terrible storms and fear of "Mooncussers" caused many a worry for sailors' poor wives.

In the 18th and 19th century, bands of robbers infested the Cape's shores. On horseback, they would lure ships in the darkest of nights using large lanterns. The ships, thinking they were following the path to safety in storms or moonless nights, would crash among the rocks near the shore. The crews would often be killed, and the ships stripped and plundered. These local pirates got the name 'Mooncussers' because they would curse the nights that had a bright light from the moon.

Rachel's husband had been killed in this manner. As a penniless, childless widow, she left Cape Cod and settled in an old fishing shack on Plymouth's Long Beach. Since Plymouth was a thriving seaport, Rachel soon again built up a reputation for predicting storms for seafaring men, and read fortunes from dawn till dusk to support herself.

However, many God-fearing townsfolk ridiculed her talent. Some were frightened by her looks and her skill. Groups of women whispered that Rachel's stained clothing, wild gray hair, and gaunt features must conjure up the devil. Others agreed and suggested she be driven out of town. Still, town fathers, teachers, wealthy folk and even ministers secretly visited her to ask advice before heading out on a sea voyage. Sea captains were known to delay a trip if "Aunt Rache" (as she was now called) predicted a storm or disaster at sea.

Chapter 2 - Sons of Mooncussers

One fine day toward the end of the 18th century, the brig *Betsy*, a ship with its captain and much of its crew from Cape Cod, stopped in Plymouth to make repairs. It was on its way to Boston delivering sugar and rum on its return from a long voyage back from the islands.

John Burgess, a sailor originally from Plymouth, told his crew about Aunt Rachael. After stopping at a local pub, the shipmates made their way to Long Beach to meet this famous soothsayer.

When they crowded around her, Rachel warned John and his crew that they should leave the ship, that it was under a curse. She warned," If you would not have the ship's bad fortune, flee her company."

John argued that the crew wasn't responsible for its construction or methods the owner used for trade.

As she continued the warning, one irate sailor, most likely well under the influence from their tavern visit, shouted, "Granny, none of your slack, or I'll put a stopper on your gab."

Aunt Rachel flew into an unexpected rage, tipping over her table screaming and swearing. She accused the sailors of being sons of Mooncussers "evil spawns of the devil",sons of murderers and thieves. The sailors were surprised and shocked by her outburst. They, in turn, swore at her, smashed some of her belongings, and broke her fence as they scrambled away from her shack amid her shrieks and shouts.

Aunt Rachel again warned John Burgess to leave the ship and these men because they were all cursed. The sailors returned to town filling a local tavern and drinking to drown their upset, spouting oaths and revenge.

That night residents woke to the sound of bells ringing. They gathered at the dock and stared aghast across the harbor to the peninsula that is Plymouth Beach. There, at the start of the beach, Rachael's shack and broken fence were ablaze, and she could be seen wrapped in a bed curtain and heard screaming curses at the sailors as her hut burned to the ground.

Chapter 3 - Rachael's Revenge

In the morning, the brig *Betsy* had been repaired and was about to set sail. Many folks gathered on the dock whispering about the evening's events. They wished to see John Burgess and the ship off. Among the crowd were the ship's owner and Aunt Rachel. Many in the crowd attempted to console her for her loss and offered food, clothing, and supplies. The ship's owner approached her offering to compensate her for her loss, including a new dwelling.

Rachel responded,

"I need it no longer, for I will soon be in a new house, one that no one, not even your wretches can burn. But you, who will console you for the loss of your Brig?"

The ship owner was surprised, as he knew the Betsy was a sturdy ship with a good captain that had endured many treacherous shoals. Rachael, knowing what he thought muttered,

"She carries a curse. She cannot swim long."

As the ship left the harbor, many found their gaze focused first on the ship, then on Rachael. The crowd gasped as the old woman leaned forward, her hands shaking, bony fingers pointing at the ship while her lips mumbled silent curses. As the ship rounded Long Beach and seemed to be heading out for the open bay, the crowd and ship owner breathed a long sigh of relief. Aunt Rachael made her way to the end of the dock and raised her arms high.

Suddenly, the ship stopped, trembled. Sails shook and the crew were seen frantically racing around the deck as the ship slowly sank until only her masthead stood out of the water. On the dock, men scrambled to rescue boats and headed toward the wreck. In all the commotion, no one noticed as Rachael pitched forward into the dark waters of Plymouth Harbor, a smile of triumph on her face.

Chapter 4 - The Rock –
Aunt Rachel's Curse

The rescuers came back with all the crew except the one who led the charge to burn down the hut. Once the excitement subsided, and the rescues were completed, Rachael's body was discovered on the shore by the Forefather's Rock as the tide receded. Residents carried her body in a solemn procession to the end of Long Beach and marked her grave with a pile of rocks that can still be seen there today.

Those who loved her wanted her to be ever able to look out at the sea, to avenge the cruelty that caused her so much pain and sadness.

The brig was eventually raised with the loss of most of her cargo. The spot where the ship sank bore a rock thereafter called "Aunt Rachael's Curse.

Note: Perhaps it is the site now known as" Bug Light", where a lighthouse was built to prevent other ships from a fate like that of the *Betsy*.

Women Before the Court in Plymouth Accused of Witchcraft

Courtesy: Collection of the
New-York Historical Society
Witch Hill, Thomas Slatterwhite Noble

Holmes vs. Sylvester 1661

William Holmes brought suit against nineteen year old Dinah Sylvester from Marshfield. He accused her of making false claims to the community that his wife Elizabeth was a witch.

Dinah claimed Holmes' wife was conversing with the devil who appeared to her in the form of a bear, and claimed that the bear was only a "stone's throw from the highway" when she observed this event. Mrs. Holmes' brother, Captain Joseph, a well-respected man in the colony, gave bond of twenty pounds sterling for his sister's appearance in the court.

Goodwife Holmes appeared before the General Court, presided by Thomas Prince, Governor, and the Court of Assistants composed of such notable men as John Alden, Josiah Winslow, Thomas Southworth and William Bradford.

When asked by the court magistrates to describe the bear's tail, Dinah testified that she could not see its tail, as its head was facing toward her. There were no other witnesses to this, nor anyone else coming forth to accuse Mrs. Holmes of witchcraft. According to the law, there had to be two or more witnesses to come forth with the accusation of witchcraft.

The Court of Assistants ruled in favor of Holmes, and declared that Dinah had to pay five pounds sterling and be publicly whipped, or else pay the court fines of William Holmes and recant her accusation. Dinah opted to recant and pay the fine.

Here are the words she was made to confess:
"To the Honorable Court assembled, whereas I have been convicted in matter of defamation concerning Goodwife Holmes, I do hereby acknowledge I have injured my neighbor, and had sinned against God in so doing, though I had entertained hard thoughts against the woman, for this had been my duty to declare my grounds, if I had any, unto some magistrate in a way of God, and not to have divulged my thoughts to others to the woman's defamation. Therefore, I do acknowledge my sin in it, and do humbly beg this Honorable Court to forgive me and all the other Christian people that I offended by it, and to promise, by the help of God, to do so no more; and although I do not remember all that the witnesses do testify, I do rather mistrust my memory and submit to the evidence. "

The mark of Dina Sylvester

Richard Sylvester, Dinah's father, paid the fine and took his daughter home. This, however, was not the end to Dinah's court appearances.

Note: "Mark" may mean Dinah was illiterate and could not write her name. Also spellings vary in the 17th century which may explain the varied spelling of her name. Look for more about Dinah Sylvester's exploits in my next book: *The Naughty Pilgrims.*

Trial of Mary Ingham 1677

The second and only other case of witchcraft in the courts of Plymouth occurred on March 6, 1677, when Mary Ingham was accused of the crime. Mary was the wife of Thomas Ingham. They resided in the town of Scituate which was part of the jurisdiction of Plymouth.

The court document reads as follows:

"Mary Ingham, thou art indicted by the name of Mary Ingham, the wife of Thomas Ingham of Scituate, for thou, not having the feare of God before thine eyes, hast, by the helpe of the Devil, in a way of witchcraft or sorcery, maliciously procured much hurt, mischieff and paine, unto the body of Mehitabel Woodworth, daughter of Walter Woodworth of Scituate, and to some others, particularly causing her to falle into violent fits, and causing her great paine unto several partes of her body at several tymes, so that the said Mehitabel hath been almost bereaved of her senses; and hath greatly languished to her much suffering thereby, and procuring of greate grieffe sorrow and charge to her parents: all which thou hast procured and done, against the law of God, and to his greate dishonor, and contrary to our Sovereign Lord the King, his crown, and dignity."

Governor Josiah Winslow presided. The General Court and the jury consisted of Thomas Huckens, John Wadsworth, John Howland (the second), Abraham

Jackson, Benjah Pratt, John Blacke, Marke Snow, Joseph Bartlett, John Richmond, Jerud Talbutt, John Foster, and Seth Pope. She was acquitted by the jury of these 12 men, but no court explanation can be found.

* * *

Historians guess this poor elderly woman may have been a hunchback and splay-footed, or had other deformities that led to superstitious neighbors accusing her of such terrible deeds.

Because neither of these cases resulted in a conviction of the accused women, some writers concluded that it discouraged other Plymouth town folk from bringing forth such cases.

As the Sylvester family discovered, the charge could backfire, causing financial hardship and humiliation to the family. In making such accusations public, without others to verify, testify and back up such a charge the results could be very costly at a time when money was scarce.

Strange Superstitions
& Practices
of the 17th & 18th Century

Ducking the Witch from Chapbooks of the
Eighteenth Century by John Ashton (1834)

Some 17th Century Practices for Protecting your Home from Witches

Witches cannot or will not enter a home:
- In which apples are stored.
- In which one door is hung upside-down.
- In which a bag of salt is stored under the bed in the master bedroom.
- In which a coffin nail, dried apple, dried clove of garlic or horseshoe is hung over each doorway.
- In which strong smelling herbs such as Hyssop, Wormwood, Mugwort, and Rosemary are hung.
- In which a horse or ox bone is buried in the foundation of a home.
- In which salt-glazed bricks are used to build a chimney and hearth.

Protecting Yourself from Witches or Countering a Witch's Spell

- Take something of the victim (urine) mix with pins and nails, and place in a corked stoneware bottle, buried upside down.
- Wear a sprig of mistletoe, a dried clove of garlic, or a piece of dried sassafras root to prevent an evil spirit from harming you.

- Put seven drops of any vegetable oil into a dish of cold water in which there is a small piece of iron. Rub your finger on the edge of the dish for three minutes in a clockwise direction. (Follow the same procedure seven times in one day at two-hour intervals to completely break the spell.)
- Toss a handful of apple seeds over your left shoulder with your right hand on a cloudless night when the moon is full.

Discovering the Identity of a Witch

If you believe food will not cook properly because a witch has cast a spell upon it, uncover her identity by placing some of that food in a fire. Heat will release the witch's imp, and she will appear at your door before anyone else arrives.

If someone in your family is being tormented by a witch, collect the urine of this poor bewitched person and bake it in a loaf of bread. Next, feed the bread to the family dog. The person or persons causing the torment will soon be revealed.

Tests to Determine an Accused Witch

Prayer Test

While it was believed that witches were incapable of reciting or speaking anything from the Bible out loud without making a mistake, victims were often tested with the recitation of the Lord's Prayer. A suspected witch could have been very nervous, illiterate, or had a speech impairment that could have caused them to stumble. However, even success did not necessarily end well for the accused. In the case of George Burroughs, while he recited the prayer perfectly while on the gallows just before execution, it was dismissed by the authorities as the "devil's trick," and he was hung as planned during the Salem Witch Trials.

Ducking Stool (not Dunking Stool)

This punishment tool was used in some of the colonies to punish "scolds" (gossip, bad-tempered or unruly woman) or suspected witches. This involved an armchair secured to a pole that suspended the chair over a body of water. The victim would be tied to the chair and repeatedly dunked in and out of the freezing water, until she confessed, repented, or was nearly drowned. The length of time the woman was submerged depended on factors such as the seriousness of the crime. It could last minutes or could be repeated continuously during an entire day.

Swimming Test

An accused witch would be brought to a nearby body of water and bound. (One case was described as the left thumb tied to the right toe and the right thumb tied to the left toe. In other cases, heavy rocks were added for weight.)The theory was that true witches rejected baptism, and therefore their body would reject the water and float to the surface. According to this belief, an innocent person would sink, and a true witch would float. The victim usually had a rope tied around her waist so she could be pulled up. This method, however, often resulted in "accidental" drowning.

Swimming the Witch
Courtesy: The Huntington Library, San Marino, CA RB25872

Witch Balls: History & Mystery

Witch balls have been used for centuries to "ward off negative energy, evil spells, witches, and bad fortune." Witch balls are popular even today. The orbs are colorful hand-blown glass, created in such a way that strands of glass left inside, resemble a web.

Many legends explain their use. However, most agree that the beautiful colors and intricate designs attract negative energy and either trap it or repel it.

One legend explains that a witch would be attracted to the beautiful glass ball, but upon touching it, her energy would be trapped inside, never to escape and cause mischief to her surroundings.

Another legend describes these spheres as "spirit balls." These have a hole on top for a spirit to fly in through. However, the spirit would become trapped inside by the glass strands within, capturing it forever.

Gazing balls are different from witch balls, but also serve the purpose of protecting a home from evil spirits. These glass spheres are larger in size and usually have one solid color. Some are placed on pedestals as lawn decorations. Unlike the Witch balls, the purpose is not to trap the witch inside. Instead, the creature would be attracted by its beauty, but because of the ball's reflective surface, the evil spirit would be repulsed by its own reflection and scared away. Gazing balls also have a positive purpose, helping a garden to grow, as well as adding to its beauty.

The colorful orbs and their traditions and legends have been around for hundreds of years. The designs, colors, and shapes have become perfected by artisans today and are displayed in many homes as decorative colorful works of art. As to the truth to their effectiveness in warding off evil spirits, that's for you to decide.

Gazing Ball 10-14

Mirrors: Magic and Myths

There are also many superstitions and legends around mirrors. In early cultures, people believed that mirrors possessed magical qualities. Some used mirrors to foretell the future. Mirrors show up in many folk tales and fairy tales. *Snow White* is a good example.

In early Christian communities, mirrors were banned because they tempted the owner to become too vain. Some held the belief that your reflection was the embodiment of your soul, and your soul could be trapped in the mirror by the devil. Pilgrim Steven Hopkins was fined on a few occasions for selling "looking glasses" to colonists. Historians attribute the fine to his overcharging the customers, while others believe it had to do with the concern of church members over the sin of vanity.

Breaking a mirror and having seven years of bad luck dates back to Roman times. Early civilizations believed that life renews itself every seven years. So if your image was captured in a shattered bit of glass, it would take seven years for your life to restore itself.

There are other antidotes for a broken mirror's curse:

- Immerse the pieces of broken glass in south-flowing water for seven hours.

- Grind the shards of broken glass into a fine powder so they do not reflect any images.
- Put broken pieces of glass in a bag and bury them.

From Africa, to southern parts of the United States, certain religious groups and cultures hold the tradition to cover their mirrors when someone dies. The custom comes from a belief that the soul of the deceased person could be trapped in the mirror, unable to complete his/her journey to the next life.

In Jewish traditions, all mirrors are covered while sitting Shivah to remind the mourners to focus on God and the deceased member, and not on vanity or their physical appearance.

Whether these superstitions and beliefs had their beginnings here, or in other parts of the world, they are part of the lore and fabric of New England.

Reflections:

As someone looking to make a positive impact in life, I ask myself, "Why would you want to write a book about witches?"

As I ponder the question, I know our words matter! Words can heal and comfort, or they can cause great pain and suffering or worse. Next I question, "Are the witch hunts really over in this modern world?" I think not!

When some seek out police officers and shoot them, just because of their uniform, is that not a witch hunt?

When teenagers target a classmate with brutal verbal and online bullying, causing them such pain that they want to kill themselves, is that not a witch hunt?

When groups in this world condemn or kill one another because of their politics, their faith, or their race, is that not a witch hunt?

When my faith tells me, "We are one body" or the course I take ends with "I am you and you are me." There is something that resonates with me about how WE (You & ME) are all part of the human condition, and horror of horrors, the persecutors are us!

But these are just stories you say. Yes, but I believe they are much more. I think in some deep place within we know **we** are part of the problem.

I love the Bible quote, Matthew 7:5 "You hypocrite, remove the wooden beam from your eye first; then you will see clearly to remove the splinter from your brother's eye."

So I will keep working on my end to be loving, peaceful, kind to others, and to "shine my light."

Diane Finn   March 2, 2017

.

Resources

Print:

Austin, Jane G. *David Alden's Daughter, and Other Stories of Colonial times*. Boston, MA: Houghton, Mifflin and Company, 1892

Austin, Jane G. *Dr. LeBaron and His Daughters a Story of the Old Colony*. Boston: Houghton, Mifflin, 1890.

Bonfanti, Leo. *Strange Beliefs, Customs, and Superstitions of New England*. Burlington, MA: Pride Publications, 1980
. Cahill, Robert Ellis. *Olde New England's Strange Superstitions*. Salem, MA: Old Saltbox Pub. House, 1990.

Chandler, Joseph R. "Superstitions of New England." *Godey's The Lady's Magazine*, March 1833, 111-12.
Aunt Rachel's Curse

Davis, William T. *History of the Town of Plymouth: With a Sketch of the Origin and Growth of Separatism. Illustrated*. Philadelphia: J.W. Lewis, 1885.

Deetz, James, and Patricia E. Scott. Deetz. *The times of Their Lives: Life, Love, and Death in Plymouth Colony*. New York: W.H. Freeman, 2000.

Goodwin, John A. *The Pilgrim Republic: An Historical Review of the Colony of New Plymouth, with Sketches of the Rise of Other New England Settlements, the History of Congregationalism, and the Creeds of the Period*. Boston: Houghton Mifflin, 1920. Newspaper Article March 1676

Hurd, D. Hamilton. *History of Essex County, Massachusetts with Biographical Sketches of Many of Its Pioneers and Prominent Men.* Philadelphia: J.W. Lewis, 1888. p, 165

Kingman, Bradford. *Epitaphs from Burial Hill, Plymouth, Massachusetts, from 1657 to 1892: With Biographical and Historical Notes.* Baltimore: Genealogical Pub., 1977.

Skinner, Charles M. *Myths & Legends of Our Own Land.* Philadelphia: J.B. Lippincott, 1896.

Stratton, Eugene Aubrey. *Plymouth Colony, Its History & People, 1620-1691.* Salt Lake City, UT: Ancestry Pub., 1986.

Terry, Eliphalet Bradford. "Witchcraft in Plymouth Colony."Bulletin of the Society of Mayflower Descendants in the state of NY, issue 6 March 1917. Pp23-25.

Websites:

Alfred, Randy. "May 19, 1780: Darkness at Noon Enshrouds New England." *Wired.* Conde Nast, 19 May 2010. https://www.wired.com/2010/05/0519New-England-dark-day/.

Andrews, Evan. "7 Bizarre Witch Trial Tests." A&E Television Networks, March 18, 2014. http://www.history.com/news/history-lists/7-bizarre-witch-trial-test

Andrews, Evan. "Remembering New England's "Dark Day"." *History.com.* A&E Television Networks, 19 May 2015. http://www.history.com/news/remembering-new-englands -dark-day.

Death Rituals and Superstitions. December 6, 2013 http://www.history.co.uk/topics/history-of-death/death-rituals-and-superstitions

Honey, Luke. "The Mysterious History of Witch Balls." Homes and Antiques. December 16, 2014 http://www.homesandantiques.com/feature/antiques/decorative /mysterious-history-witch-balls.

Horrigan, John. "The Dark Day Over Olde New England." What Caused New England's Dark Day? n.d. http://www.johnhorrigan.com/darkday.html.

Legends of Mooncussers http://www.mooncusserstavern.com/about-mooncussers-tavern/

Thomas, Ryan. "10 Tests For Guilt at the Salem Witch Trials .July 27, 2012. http://listverse.com/2012/07/27/10-tests-for-guilt-used-at-the-salem-witch-trials/History

.

Sanofsky, Josh. "The Meaning of Mirrors in Folklore and Superstition." Week In Weird. August 27, 2012. http://weekinweird.com/2012/08/27/time-reflection-mirrors-folklore-superstition/.

Witchball Legends, Moonlight Go, 2014
http://www.sunnyreflections.com/witchballs-legends/

Young, Eric G. "Mirror, Mirror On The Wall - A History Of Mirrors; Their Meaning In Myth, Legend, Folk Tales & Superstition." Jun 10, 2015.
http://www.mythbeliefs.info/2015/06/mirror-mirror-on-wall-history-of.html